The Sleepover Club

*Have you been
invited to all these
sleepovers?*

Sleepover Girls on the Range

by Fiona Cummings

The Sleepover Club ® is a
registered trademark of HarperCollins*Publishers* Ltd

First published in Great Britain by Collins in 2000
Collins is an imprint of HarperCollins*Publishers* Ltd
77-85 Fulham Palace Road, Hammersmith,
London, W6 8JB

The HarperCollins website address is
www.**fire**and**water**.com

1 3 5 7 9 8 6 4 2

Text copyright © Fiona Cummings 2000

Original series characters, plotlines
and settings © Rose Impey 1997

ISBN 0 00675499-6

The author asserts the moral right to
be identified as the author of the work.

Printed and bound in Great Britain by
Caledonian International Book Manufacturing Ltd,
Glasgow G64

Sleepover Kit List

1. Sleeping bag
2. Pillow
3. Pyjamas or a nightdress
4. Slippers
5. Toothbrush, toothpaste, soap etc
6. Towel
7. Teddy
8. A creepy story
9. Food for a midnight feast:
   chocolate, crisps, sweets, biscuits.
   In fact anything you like to eat.
10. Torch
11. Hairbrush
12. Hair things like a bobble or hairband,
    if you need them
13. Clean knickers and socks
14. Change of clothes for the next day
15. Sleepover diary and membership card

CHAPTER ONE

Yeehah! If it ain't my perdy liddle friend. Let's mosey on down to the OK Corral pardn'r and round up them there horses.

Hey, don't look at me like that! All I meant was "do you fancy coming down to the stables with me?" I've kind of got this thing about the Wild West at the moment. The others are used to it now. In fact they're so used to it that I'm driving them all crazy. Especially Fliss. She keeps saying:

"Look Lyndz, if you don't drop that stupid accent soon, I'm going to ram that stetson down your *perdy liddle* throat!"

Now that's not very nice, is it? Particularly since the others were just as bad as me last week. If I remember rightly, it was Frankie who threw herself into the Wild West theme big time. And she even got everybody dressing up in cowboy gear into the bargain. You know how she organises everybody. Once she's got an idea in her head, you daren't argue with her!

You're looking a bit puzzled. You must have heard what happened down at the stables, surely? What! You mean you haven't? I thought *everybody* knew about that by now. Kenny certainly hasn't stopped talking about it, and you know what a motormouth she is. And now I come to think about it, Fliss is pretty pleased with herself too. And when she's like that, she usually tells the whole world!

I can't believe that *none* of them have told you about our latest sleepover adventure. But that's great, because it means that *I* get to tell you about it. And after all, it was because of me that we got involved in the first place. That goes without saying really, doesn't it? As my mum keeps saying, "If horses are involved, Lyndsey Collins will be in the thick of it!"

I can't help it if I love horses, can I? You know where you are with horses, which is more than you can say for people. Take my four brothers for example (I wish someone would, they drive me mad!). Sometimes they treat me like dirt and expect me to run around clearing up after them. And sometimes they're OK and help me out of a jam. But you can never predict what they're going to be like. Now, horses are never like that.

Is that the phone? Hang on, I'd better go and answer it.

"Hello? Oh hi, Rosie. Yeah we're just going down to the stables now... You're all coming too? Cool! Yeah, you're right, no M&Ms! ... It was class, wasn't it? Yeah, the best yet... No, I won't forget. OK, we'll meet you down there. Bye."

That was Rosie. Ever since our last sleepover adventure, she's been going to the stables too. Not that she does much when she's there – she just sits and watches Bramble and Marvel munching away at the grass. And sometimes she watches her brother Adam, who does his Riding for the Disabled there. But the *real* attraction of the stables, as far as the others are concerned, is that we know we won't be disturbed by our rivals the M&Ms. Because we have just got one over them in a major supertastic way!

Oh hey, sorry. My mum always tells me off for that – for coming into a story half-way through. "For goodness sake, Lyndz, start at the beginning!" she tells me. So that's what I'm going to do now. It'll pass the time as we walk to the stables.

OK, well – do you remember when Mrs McAllister's stables burnt down? I know we've had a lot of sleepover adventures since then, so I'll remind you what happened. We were so worried about Mrs McA having to close her stables down for good that we went into fundraising overdrive. Our first attempt was a flop, thanks to those stupid M&Ms. But then I came up with the idea of a Stable Fun Day, which was brill.

Unfortunately, the only thing people remember about it now is Fliss screaming her head off on a runaway horse! Her picture ended up on the front page of the *Leicester Mercury* and they started a campaign to save the stables. And that's where Sita Chandri stepped in. She's this hot-shot business-woman from around here. She read about the campaign and stumped up the dosh to rebuild Mrs McAllister's stables. Cool, eh? Fliss takes all the credit for everything of course, but then we're used to that!

Well anyway, since the fire Mrs McAllister has had to keep her horses down at Mr Brocklehurst's farm. And that's where I went to see her a couple of weeks ago. When I got there, she was really excited.

"The builders say my new stable block will be finished next week, Lyndsey. Isn't that wonderful?" she grinned. Her eyes were shining, and I thought for a minute that she was going to cry. But I knew it was just because she was happy. I felt pretty top-banana myself. It seemed ages since the horses had had a proper home of their own.

"They ought to have a stable-warming party or something!" I chuckled. Alfie, my very favourite horse, came strolling over to us. He stretched his neck over the fence and started to nuzzle my pocket to see if I'd brought him some of his favourite mints.

"Hey Alfie, would you like a party?" I asked, patting his face.

"Well, it's funny you should mention that, Lyndsey," said Mrs McAllister seriously. "Because I certainly want to do something special to mark the re-opening of my stables—"

"A party!" I started to jump around. "Cool!"

"Well, maybe not a party exactly. I had more of a public Open Day in mind," she admitted. "Just to show that the stables are fully operational again. A lot of people cancelled their lessons after the fire because they thought my premises were unsafe, even though it was only the stable block that was damaged. I really need to build my business up again now, as my bank manager will remind me yet *again* when I meet with him tomorrow." She grimaced, and a cloud seemed to pass over her face. But she soon brightened up again. "An Open Day should be a good opportunity to remind everyone that I'm really and truly back in business, don't you think? Even my bank manager has to agree with that!"

"An Open Day? OK!" I nodded. I mean, it didn't sound as much fun as a party, but it should be fun all the same. "It worked when we had the Stable Fun Day, didn't it?"

"Well yes, you could say that!" Mrs McAllister looked dubious. "But I thought we could do something a bit different this time. I'm not sure what yet."

"Hmm – I'm sure we can think of something…" My mind started to race.

Mrs McAllister looked at me.

"Actually, you needn't worry about the Open Day at all, Lyndsey," she said quickly.

I must have looked disappointed, because she started to laugh.

"You needn't look like that. It's just that I've got something very special for you to think about."

"Oh?"

"I haven't forgotten how hard you and your friends worked to raise money for my stables," she told me seriously. "And I've never really had a proper chance to thank you for it."

I didn't know what to say, so I just blushed and shrugged my shoulders and mumbled, "You don't have to do that."

"Oh, but I do, Lyndsey," Mrs McAllister continued, "because if it hadn't been for you lot, Sita would never have come along and put up the money for the stable block. I've a lot to thank you for, and so have the horses!"

As if on cue Alfie began to whinny, and Marvel, Bramble and Trojan came over to join him at the fence. Mrs McAllister and I cracked up laughing.

"You see, they know what we're talking about!"

When we'd made a fuss of the horses, Mrs McAllister went on:

"So I'd like you to think of a special treat that I can give you and your friends. Is there anything you have in mind?"

I thought hard – for about a minute – and

then I grinned.

"Well there is something. But I'll have to ask the others first."

I had thought of something so mind-blowingly wonderful, it was like a hot fudge sundae and a knickerbocker glory all rolled into one. All I had to do now was persuade the others. And I knew at least one of them wouldn't agree with me at all...

CHAPTER TWO

All the way home from the stables, my mind was whizzing with plans for this special treat. I couldn't think about anything else. It was going to be so different from anything we'd ever done before, but at the same time so totally cool! I knew that I had to share it with the others as soon as I got in.

Well that was the plan anyway, but I couldn't get a look in on the phone. First, one of Dad's teacher colleagues rang about some meeting or other. Yawn, yawn, bor-ing! Then one of Mum's midwife friends called and they talked for hours about every baby they'd ever delivered. Double boring with chocolate on top. Then *just* when I thought the phone was free, Stuart got on it and started talking to someone in a really soppy voice. Tom and I kept sneaking up behind him and singing:

"Stuart's got a girlfriend!"

Stuart was not pleased.

Anyway, when the phone was finally free (after Stuart had hogged it for about three hours) I pounced on it.

"No chance, Lyndsey Collins!" laughed Mum, whisking the receiver out of my hand. "Have you seen the time? It's time you were in bed, my girl!"

"Aw Mum, just a quick one?" I pleaded.

"No way!" Mum held firm. "I know your quick phone calls. You'd be talking for an hour at least. Now scoot!"

I had all that exciting news bubbling inside me and I had to keep it there until the next day!! It's a wonder I managed to sleep at all.

The next morning I was up with the larks and desperate to get to school to see the others. But Ben took forever to get ready, and then Spike was sick and needed to be changed before we could set off. Then Tom decided that he needed a lift too. So by the time we finally made it to my school, the bell was ringing and everyone else was in the classroom.

"Don't forget you've got the dentist this afternoon," Mum called out after me. "I'll pick you up at two."

I flew inside just as everyone was settling down for the register. Mrs Weaver's a bit of a stickler for us keeping quiet while she takes it, so there was no chance of me speaking to the others. I just managed to mouth to them:

"I've got some great news. I'll tell you at break time."

And let me tell you, break time couldn't come soon enough, because our first lesson was maths and I just couldn't get my head round it at all. Neither could Kenny, mind you – she spent all her time flicking bits of rubber at the M&Ms, then pretending to be hard at work whenever they turned round.

When the bell finally went, we all piled out into the playground. Well, the rest of us did. Fliss was messing about somewhere inside, probably doing her hair or something.

"Come on Lyndz, spill! What's this great news then?" asked Frankie.

I loved seeing their expectant faces looking at me like that. And I loved milking the moment too.

"Shouldn't we wait for Fliss?" I asked innocently. "You know what she's like if she's left out."

We all turned towards the door, just in time to see Fliss appearing.

"Come on, Fliss!" shouted Kenny sharply. "We're all waiting for you."

Fliss looked very flustered and started to run towards us. But suddenly this leg appeared from behind the door. Fliss saw it too late, tried to jump over it, but couldn't. The next thing we knew, she was sprawling on the ground.

"Fliss! Are you all right?" We all ran towards her.

"Enjoy your trip, Felicity?" cackled a voice behind us. We didn't even need to look up to know that that was Emma Hughes, M&M Number One.

"I'm going to get you for this!" Kenny yelled at Emma and M&M Number Two Emily as they ran off cackling down the playground.

"I should have known," Frankie sighed. "They're still trying to pay us back for what we did to them in the scavenger hunt, aren't they?"

Now you *must* remember what happened in the scavenger hunt! We're still laughing about it. We didn't think the M&Ms were going to take part in the hunt at all, so you could have knocked us down with a feather when they turned up with their mates. They were determined to win the prize, you see. We were seriously worried when we thought they actually *might* win the thing. We came up with loads of cunning plans to try to put them off the scent, but it was Fliss's mum, of all people, who managed to do the job for us! They got disqualified from the competition completely. So that's why they were planning their pay-back time.

Anyway, just at that moment I wasn't concerned about their stupid revenge. I was more concerned about Fliss.

"We'd better get someone to look at you," I told her gently, helping her to her feet.

Poor Fliss – she was crying but trying not to. Both her palms were grazed and she had a nasty gash to her right knee which blood was starting to trickle from.

"Ouch, that looks nasty!" said Rosie sympathetically.

Kenny cast her eye over it. "Well you certainly need to get all the grit out of there," she said in her best doctor's voice. "But you'll live!"

"Th...thanks a lot!" sobbed Fliss, and hobbled inside with the rest of us supporting her.

Well, so much for me telling the others my news. By the time Fliss was sorted out it was the end of break time. So that meant I had to wait until after lunch before I could tell them. We don't all eat our lunch together, you see. At our school the people who bring packed lunches can't eat with the people who have school dinners. Crazy I know, but there you go. And as Kenny isn't really fussy about what she eats, she always has a cooked lunch. We tease her about eating sheeps' eyeballs and stuff but she just says, "Yum, yum!" and licks her lips!

Anyway, as I wanted to tell all the others my news at the same time, I had to wait. And by the time we were all settled down on the grass together, I was absolutely *bursting* with it.

"You know that I had something to tell you? Well, Mrs McAllister is planning something special for the opening of her new stable block—" I began.

"And she wants us to plan another Stable Fun Day?" asked Rosie. "Cool!"

"Well not exactly," I tried to continue. "I think she's planning more of an Open Day. But the thing is—"

"I'm not getting on a horse again!" snapped Fliss.

"You don't have to, Fliss, because—"

Suddenly there were gales of laughter from the bushes behind us.

"You got a bit carried away the last time you were on a horse, didn't you Felicity?"

It was the Gruesome Twosome! They'd only been earwigging, hadn't they?

"Right that's it!" Kenny leapt up and dashed into the bushes.

Branches snapped, and there were stifled screams and shouts of "Gerroff, you moron!" Then we heard the M&Ms scrambling out through the back of the bushes and running away.

When Kenny emerged, she was holding a fistful of hair and looking very pleased with herself.

"That should keep them quiet for a while!"

The rest of us were kind of shocked. I mean, there was enough hair there to stuff a cushion. The M&Ms would have bald patches for sure.

"*Kenny!*" Even Frankie seemed shocked. "I mean, pulling their hair out, that's a bit strong, isn't it?"

Kenny snorted with laughter. "I didn't pull it out, dumbo! It just got caught on all the branches as they tried to run away from me."

There's nothing we like better than getting one over on our rivals! Except perhaps...

"My news! I almost forgot!" I leapt up. "Mrs McAllister said that…"

"Come on, girls!" Mrs Weaver was heading towards us. "Didn't you hear the bell? Hurry up, you're going to be late!"

Talk about bad timing! Was I *ever* going to tell my friends my news, or was I going to end up having this treat on my own?

It didn't help that I had to leave school early for the dentist, so I didn't even have the chance to tell them about it later. Talk about fed up!

When I got to the van Mum laughed.

"Why the long face, Lyndz? Bad day?"

I nodded. "Something like that. I've got this great news to tell the others, but I just don't think I'm ever going to have the chance."

Mum gave me a funny look. She knows that when I have "great news" it usually leads to trouble one way or another.

"Well, can't you tell them tomorrow?"

"Not if it's anything like today," I explained. "The M&Ms always spoil things for us."

"OK," Mum said. "What about if you invite your friends round after school? You can tell them then."

"YEESS!!" I punched the air. "Thanks Mum!"

I couldn't *wait* to tell the others. Thinking about it even got me through the dentist. As soon as I got home, I sat by the phone until I was sure that the others would be home too. Then I dialled Frankie's number.

"Hi Frankie – it's me, Lyndz. If you want to hear about my news you've got to come round to my place tomorrow after school. OK?"

I didn't give her chance to ask any questions. I just said "bye" and put the phone down. And I did the same with the others. Those were the shortest phone conversations I'd ever had with my friends.

The next day they were all intrigued by the mystery.

"Can't you tell us what this is about, Lyndz, please?" they begged. But I wasn't going to give in. By the time Mum came to collect us all from school, they were really wound up about it!

"Come on Lyndz, we're here now," Rosie said as soon as we'd leapt out of the van at my place. "Won't you please tell us what all this is about?"

"Yes!" I told them triumphantly. "But only after we've all dressed up."

Well, they didn't need telling twice. I have this fab box of dressing-up clothes, you see. And we all love to pile in and don all these weird and wonderful costumes. Fliss reached in and grabbed the bride's dress (surprise, surprise), Rosie put on a clown's outfit, Frankie dressed up as a gypsy, Kenny borrowed my leather chaps and cowboy hat, and I turned myself into a fire-fighting princess!

We all charged outside and chased round like loonies. Unfortunately, Ben heard us and wanted to join in. So just to keep him quiet we had a mock-battle, hiding behind bushes and leaping out to ambush him. Then we pretended we were in the jungle, climbing trees to escape from the poisonous snakes which I convinced everyone were slithering about on the ground. We must have looked really wild sitting amongst the branches in our dressing-up clothes.

When Mum had called Ben inside, we collapsed on to the grass, panting for breath.

"Hey Lyndz, we almost forgot about your surprise!" squealed Fliss suddenly, half-sitting up and squinting into the sunshine.

"Oh yes, the Open Day!" Rosie reminded me.

"Well, that's not the surprise actually," I reminded them. "I think Mrs McAllister wants to keep that a bit, you know, low-key."

"Boring, more like!" Kenny chimed in.

"She just wants to show everyone that the stables are open again, so that she can get her business back," I explained.

"Well if she wants to do that, she should make it *fun*," said Frankie, suddenly sitting up. You could tell by her voice that she was serious.

"What do you mean?" I asked.

"The more exciting the Open Day is, the more people are going to want to go to her for riding lessons," Frankie explained patiently.

"Yeah, remember how many people turned up for the Stable Fun Day?" Rosie reminded us.

"But I don't think she really wants to involve the horses again," I tried to explain. "After what happened last time."

We all looked at Fliss, but she just started picking blades of grass from her dress.

"The horses needn't be involved at all." Frankie was getting excited now. "We could have a horsey theme and just go with that."

"What, like the Wild West, maybe?" I asked. Dad's always watching those old cowboy movies on TV.

"Yeah, good one!" Frankie went on, her eyes blazing. "There could be a Wild West fancy-dress competition for children—"

"And for adults!" Rosie chipped in. "Mum always fancies herself as a bit of a cowgirl. She goes line-dancing now."

"Yeah, she goes with my mum," Fliss suddenly piped up. "Maybe we could have a bit of line-dancing at this Open Day! I'm sure our mums could persuade some of their friends to come along."

"That's a good idea, Fliss," Frankie nodded. "Because then Mrs McAllister could show off her stables to people who might not even know about them."

"And we could have real cowboy food!" I giggled. "Round a big campfire like they always have in those films!"

"Yes!"

We started to dance around. This was going to be brilliant!

Then it hit me. We weren't supposed to be organising Mrs McAllister's Open Day at all.

"But guys, the Open Day isn't really anything to do with us!" I stopped jumping around.

"It isn't?" They all looked surprised.

"No!" I laughed. "As well as having the Open Day for everybody, Mrs McAllister wants to give a special treat to just the five of us. It's her way of saying thank you to us for helping raise money for the stables last time."

"Great! What is it?" asked Frankie.

I took a deep breath. This was the moment I'd been waiting for!

29

"Well, what about a sleepover? In one of the barns? We'll be like real cowboys – it'll be so cool! What do you say?"

No-one said anything. They just stared at me.

CHAPTER
THREE

Fliss was the first to speak.

"A sleepover in a b…barn? I don't think so, Lyndz."

She looked round at the others for encouragement. Now I had expected problems from Fliss, but not from everyone else. I thought they'd be thrilled.

"You mean, you want us to sleep where Alfie sleeps?" asked Rosie incredulously. "What if he tramples us or something?"

"And wouldn't it be a bit, you know, stinky?" sniffed Frankie. "You know what a mess it is when you're mucking out."

I started to laugh.

"De-err!" I put my finger to my head. "We'd be sleeping in an empty *barn*, dumbos, not a *stable*! We'd probably give Alfie nightmares if we pitched down our sleeping bags with him!"

"Well, it sounds brill to me!" Kenny suddenly leapt up and flicked the brim of her cowboy hat with her finger. Then she put on a terrible American accent. "There'll be a wild time in that ol' barn when the Sleepover Club move into town. Yes siree!"

"I'm still not sure," Fliss mumbled. "It'll be kind of spooky in a barn at night, won't it?"

"Mrs McAllister does have lights in there, you know," I explained. "She's had a full security system fitted too, and her house is right next door to the barn anyway. Come on Fliss, it'll be as safe as anything. What do the rest of you think?"

"I think it's a brilliant idea. Count me in!" Kenny came to stand next to me. "What about you, Frankie? You're not wimping out as well, are you?"

"Nope." Frankie stood up and came over

to join us. "As long as the horses aren't sleeping over with us, you can count me in too!"

"And me!" Rosie leapt up. "It'll be great, really different. It's a brilliant idea, Lyndz!"

Phew – that was a relief!

"Well Fliss, are you in or out? Because you're definitely outvoted, four to one," Kenny told her firmly. "So we'll be having this sleepover whether you're there or not!"

Now as you probably know, Fliss hates being left out more than anything else in the world. She reluctantly got to her feet.

"OK, I'm in," she agreed. "But I'm not really happy about it."

"Nice one, Fliss!"

We grabbed each other in a circle and started to dance round, faster and faster. By the time we'd collapsed in a heap on the grass, even Fliss was smiling again!

"So," panted Frankie as we were all getting our breath back. "What did Mrs McAllister say when you suggested your great plan to her?"

"Well," I admitted slowly. "I haven't

actually mentioned it to her yet. I wanted to clear it with you lot first."

"Oh?" The others looked at me wide-eyed. Fliss began to smile.

"Well, I guess we'd better see what she has to say before we get so carried away," she grinned. "Hadn't we?"

She was right of course. So we all agreed to meet down at the horses' temporary home, Mr Brocklehurst's farm, after school the following afternoon.

Now to be honest with you, I'd never given Mrs McAllister's reaction a second thought. She'd said she wanted to give us a treat, hadn't she? And it wasn't as if I was asking for the Crown Jewels or anything. But as my friends' reaction to the sleepover hadn't exactly been what I'd expected, by the time we met up at the farm the next day I was a bag of nerves.

"Perhaps you're right, Fliss," I told her when we were all together. "Maybe this sleepover idea isn't such a good one."

"Don't be silly. It's brilliant!" Kenny reassured me. "It's going to be mega! Hi

34

there, Mrs McAllister!"

She waved across the field. Mrs McAllister was coming towards us, leading Bramble.

"I...I'll just wait over there," stammered Fliss when she caught sight of the horse. Fliss has been down there loads of times since the Stable Fun Day, but she still gets all twitchy whenever she gets too close to one of the horses.

"Don't be silly Fliss, you're staying right here!" Kenny grabbed her by the elbow and held on to her.

"Well, it's nice to see you. Have you come to help out?" Mrs McAllister asked pleasantly enough. But I could tell that she wasn't quite herself.

"Well, erm..." I mumbled.

"Lyndz was telling us about the stable block being almost finished and about your plans for the Open Day," Frankie explained.

"Oh yes?" Mrs McAllister didn't sound too enthusiastic.

Frankie started to speak again, but was drowned out by the crunch of gravel as a car drove through the gate. Bramble strained a little at the sound and tossed his head, making Mrs McAllister work to control him. Fliss looked terrified, as though Bramble was going to break free and trample her. I turned to see who had arrived, but the car must have driven behind one of the outbuildings.

"What was that you were saying?" Mrs McAllister asked when she'd calmed Bramble down.

"I was just saying what a wonderful opportunity the Open Day will be to show everyone what a fun place your stables are," Frankie continued confidently. "And if you have a Wild West theme or something, people can dress up and really feel part of it."

"Maybe you could have a fancy-dress competition," Fliss smiled.

"Well, I don't know…" Mrs McAllister sounded doubtful.

"And you can maybe have line-dancing," continued Rosie.

"And food cooked round a campfire," I chipped in, forgetting that we hadn't come to talk about the Open Day at all.

"And what about a lassoing competition?"

suggested Kenny. "Like they do on those cowboy films. I bet that's cool!"

We all nodded.

"That's a great idea!" I told her. "You didn't mention that yesterday."

"I've only just thought of it," Kenny told me proudly.

Mrs McAllister looked kind of annoyed.

"Oh, so you have discussed this already, have you?" she asked sharply.

I was kind of taken aback by her tone. And so were the others, because they all started to look very uncomfortable.

"Look girls, it's really kind of you to come up with all these suggestions." Mrs McAllister's voice softened a little. "But as I told Lyndsey the other day, this Open Day isn't going to be that kind of occasion. I'm going to show people round the new stable block, and maybe organise a pony trek to whet people's appetites. Business has been really bad and I need to build it up again – fast. All your ideas would cost money, and that's something that I just don't have to spare at the moment. My bank manager told

me that in no uncertain terms the other day.
I don't think he'd be very impressed if he
thought I was going to lavish money on some
big promotional extravaganza. I really am
very sorry."

She turned and walked Bramble back
down the field.

"Well, so much for that, then," sighed
Frankie. "And we didn't even get to ask her
about the sleepover."

"What sleepover?" asked a voice.

We spun round to see who it was. Behind
us was standing this tiny woman with pretty
coffee-coloured skin and the most fabulous
straight black hair which hung down to her
waist like a waterfall.

"Hello, I'm Sita Chandri," she said, holding
out a petite hand. "I've just popped over to
show Margaret – Mrs McAllister – some
paperwork." She was holding a bundle of
papers between her slim fingers, which had
the most perfectly shaped, red painted nails
you've ever seen.

We were all kind of awestruck and nobody
knew what to say.

"I hope you don't mind, but I couldn't help overhearing your plans for the Open Day," she continued, smiling. "I think that is exactly what the stables needs. It will be lively and fun and will appeal to everybody. I'm sure it will bring in lots of business too."

"I don't think Mrs McAllister was too enthusiastic, though," Kenny said sadly.

"I think Margaret is just a little cautious," Mrs Chandri told us. "I think her idea of a pony trek is a good one too. Let me just go and talk to her. I'll be back in a minute."

She climbed nimbly over the fence and ran down the field towards Mrs McAllister, her hair flowing behind her.

"Did you see those nails?" Rosie exclaimed excitedly.

"And did you see what kind of jeans she was wearing?" marvelled Fliss. "Those cost an absolute fortune! She must be *rolling* in money!"

"Mum said that she built her Spice Company up from nothing," Frankie told us. "And now she's one of the wealthiest women in Britain."

"Crikey!"

We all looked to where she was talking to Mrs McAllister. Mrs Chandri was waving her arms about enthusiastically, but Mrs McAllister had her back to us so it was hard to see her reaction.

"I don't think anything will budge Mrs McAllister," Fliss predicted.

Mrs McAllister and Sita Chandri slowly started walking towards us across the field. I hardly dared breathe.

"Well, we've got good news," Mrs Chandri smiled when she reached us. "Margaret has agreed that your ideas for the Open Day are bound to increase interest in her stables. I've agreed to go over the financial side of things and make sure that enough money is raised to cover expenditure—"

"So the Open Day is on, then?" asked Kenny.

"It most certainly is – *if*, and this is a *big* if…" Mrs Chandri suddenly looked seriously at us. "*If*… you girls are prepared to help to organise it. Margaret and I will help too, of course, but we can't do everything. I know it

40

will be tough with your schoolwork, so I would rather you spoke up now if you think it's going to be too much for you."

We all looked at each other.

"It'll be great!"

"We can do it!"

"We're kind of used to organising things now!"

Mrs Chandri smiled.

"Well I'm very pleased to hear it. Now, what was that you mentioned earlier? Something about a sleepover, wasn't it?"

Crazy though it sounds, I'd almost forgotten about that.

"Well last time... here... treat..." I just couldn't get my words out. I took a deep breath.

"That is, Mrs McAllister said that she wanted to give us a treat for helping with the fundraising for the stables. And we've thought about it, and what we'd really, *really* like is a sleepover in the barn. If that's all right."

Fliss snorted, but the others were silent like me. We were all holding our breath, waiting anxiously to see what Mrs McAllister's reaction was.

"Hmm, I hadn't expected that, I must admit," she said at last. "What do you think?" She turned to Mrs Chandri.

Smiling, Mrs Chandri said, "Well, you know I always believe in incentives and rewards for good work. If you really want this sleepover, then it will be a good incentive for you to work really hard to organise the Open Day. And it will also be a good reward for you to enjoy when it is finished."

"So that's a yes?" I asked excitedly.

"That's down to Margaret." Mrs Chandri looked over to Mrs McAllister.

"OK then, you can have your sleepover," said Mrs McAllister. "As long as I don't have any disasters to contend with during the Open Day. No runaway horses, OK?!"

"OK!" we all agreed.

When Mrs McAllister and Mrs Chandri had left us and were walking back down the field, we started squealing and hugging each other. Fliss wasn't quite as enthusiastic as the rest of us, but at least she joined in.

It did cross my mind then that something *always* goes wrong whenever we organise anything. And something told me that this time would be no exception...

CHAPTER FOUR

Whenever the Sleepover Club is involved in organising anything, we usually take it at a leisurely pace. We munch a few choccy biccies, slurp some Coca-Cola and come up with some crazy suggestions. *Then* we get serious. Not this time. No siree! This time we had Mrs Chandri to reckon with. She was like a mega-planning whirlwind and there was no stopping her. The next day she got us all squashed into Mrs McAllister's office, put a pad on her knee, took a pen in her hand, and she was off.

"How does Saturday 28th sound for the Open Day?" she asked, casting her eye over a calendar.

Not waiting for a reply she continued:

"That gives us plenty of time to get everything organised. Can you girls do the posters? But check everything out first. The fancy-dress idea is good, but how would a lassoing competition work? And where will you get your line-dance caller? Details, details. Check it out. And the food. Do you know anyone who can cook the food round the fire? It's a nice idea, but it might just be easier to hire a burger van."

The woman never seemed to draw breath. We just stared at her with our mouths open.

"Right, that gives you plenty to think about, doesn't it?" She snapped the top on her pen and smiled at us. "Don't look so worried, you'll be fine. You can ring me up if you run into any problems – here's my number."

She scribbled a number on a piece of paper and handed it over to Kenny.

"No pressure, but I could do with the

poster as soon as possible," she smiled at us again. "If it's OK, I'll have copies printed off and we can put them up. Right then, see you soon!"

She got up and showed us out of the office. *Mrs McAllister's* office. I looked round at Mrs McAllister, who just smiled sympathetically.

"Crikey, talk about slave-driver!" shrieked Kenny as we walked towards the gate. "Check this, sort out that! What does she think we are?"

"Blimmin' robots, that's what," sighed Rosie. "And overworked ones at that!"

"I guess she's only making sure that nothing goes wrong," said Fliss quietly.

"Yeah, you're right," I admitted. "We have got into a few messes in the past when we've tried to organise stuff, haven't we?"

The others agreed, but I could sense that Frankie was still pretty wound up.

"Well, we're going to show Sita Chandri that we're quite capable of organising things ourselves," she told us firmly. "We can't afford to stuff up this time. The reputation of the Sleepover Club is at stake!"

Well, that sounded a bit dramatic, but that's Frankie for you.

"So we've got to think about this lassoing competition," she continued sharply, going into 'Sita' mode. "And when do your mums go line-dancing, Fliss, Rosie?"

"Thursday," Fliss told her. "Isn't that right, Rosie?"

Rosie nodded.

"OK, we'll have to go ourselves to check it out and to try to persuade the caller to perform at the Open Day," Frankie told us firmly. "And get your thinking caps on to find someone who can cook round the fire for us. Burger van!" she snorted. "Cowboys didn't go to burger vans, did they?"

We walked the rest of the way home in silence. Like I've said before, once Frankie's in a mood there's no point arguing with her.

Seeing as I live nearest to the farm and a little further out than any of the others, they all waited at my place for their parents to collect them. As we waited, we sat in the garden and pondered some more about the Open Day. I couldn't help wishing that I'd

47

kept my big mouth shut about the whole thing. Not about the sleepover of course, but that seemed *ages* away now. We had so much to get through before we could enjoy that. And the way we were going, we'd certainly deserve it!

As the rest of us were pondering, Kenny picked up a piece of Mum's old washing line, which was kicking about in the garden. She tied a moveable knot in one end so that the end formed a noose. Then she started to swing it round above her head.

"What are you doing, Kenny?" Fliss asked.

"I'm practising lassoing, what does it look like?" she snapped back.

"So-rree!" mumbled Fliss.

Kenny swung the lasso round some more. Then, when she'd just gained enough momentum, she threw the end with the loop out into the garden. To start with, she didn't get it right at all, and let the whole thing go. Once it got tangled in one of the bushes – the other time it just missed Buster, my dog. Buster ran inside in fright, but Kenny's eyes started gleaming.

"That's what I need – some sort of target!"

She looked around. Ben was charging about down at the bottom of the garden, pretending to be a dinosaur. (Don't ask. He is only four. *And* he's a boy!)

"Hey, Ben!" she called out. "Can you come here a minute?"

"Kenny, you can't!" I yelped. "You'll strangle him!"

Ben came running up to us, thrilled to be joining in.

"You look like a pretty good cowboy to me!" Kenny told him. Ben beamed. "I'm just learning how to lasso – can I borrow your rocking horse to practise on?"

"If I can 'so too!" he agreed.

So we trooped upstairs and carried Ben's rocking horse into the garden. It made a pretty good target. It sort of moved in the wind a bit so you had to really concentrate to try to lasso it. Not that I was any good. Ben was better than me, but Kenny really got into it.

"That was great!" she gasped, finally flopping down on the grass next to me. "We need something like the rocking horse for the competition. Everyone can have three goes to try to lasso it, then we keep moving it further and further back. So the person who manages to lasso it at the furthest distance wins the prize."

"Brill!" we all congratulated her. "That's one problem solved, eh Frankie?"

"Sure!" Frankie agreed. "But there's still a lot for us to think about."

And it looked like we were going to have to think about it by ourselves, because Kenny's dad had just arrived, followed by Andy, Fliss's mum's fiancé. It was time for the others to go home.

"Don't forget to ask your parents about line-dancing," hissed Frankie before they left. "And remember that we need someone to cook for us at the Open Day too."

When the others had gone I flopped down on the settee in the lounge. I just needed to think about things for a while. Dad and Tom were watching some old cowboy movie, which seemed sort of appropriate. I can never work out what's going on in those films. Everyone looks the same, and all they seem to do is shoot people and ride horses. But I love the horse bit, so I settled down to watch the film too.

When it had finished, Dad said, "Well, they don't make films like they used to!"

"Thank goodness!" I muttered under my breath. Give me *Toy Story 2* any day!

"Hey you, don't be so rude!" Dad laughed. "It's every man's secret fantasy to be a cowboy, didn't you know that?"

No I didn't, and it was very interesting. *Very interesting indeed!*

The next morning I rushed into the playground to find the others.

"Hey, you guys!" I yelled as soon as I spotted them. "I've had an idea. Last night Dad was watching that Western on TV."

"So was mine," Frankie said.

"And mine," Kenny agreed. "Although he kept pretending he wasn't."

"Well, Dad said that it's every man's fantasy to be a cowboy," I continued. "So maybe our dads would like to help out at our

Open Day. It'd be like making their dreams come true!"

"Hardly!" Frankie snorted. "It won't exactly be riding wild on the prairies, will it?"

"But if they took charge of the food," I suggested, "it'd be like those big campfires they have. We could even let them tell some of their favourite cowboy stories!"

"Yeah, and send everyone to sleep!" grinned Rosie. I was kind of glad that she was getting into the spirit of it, because I'd suddenly felt a bit bad talking about our dads when her dad doesn't live with her any more. Neither does Fliss's, but at least she's got Andy.

"It does sound a good idea," Frankie agreed. "But we ought to ask them when they're all together. They're less likely to say 'no' then."

"Good thinking, Batman!" I grinned.

As we were wondering when would be a good time to ask them, Fliss piped up:

"Are you all coming to the line-dancing tomorrow? I can't wait. I'm going to dress up in my jeans and cowboy boots and everything."

We all rolled our eyes. Fliss manages to turn *everything* into a fashion parade.

"Yeah, Mum said she'd come along too if that's OK," I told the others.

"'Course!" giggled Rosie, "The more the merrier. I just hope I can manage all the steps. Mum says they're a bit complicated at first."

"We'll be brill!" Kenny rocked her feet and did those turns you see line-dancers doing on the TV. "They won't know what's hit them when they see us!"

"That's what we're worried about!" Frankie and I spluttered together.

As it was, when we did get to the line-dance evening, we felt a bit over-awed by it all. Fliss didn't look out of place at all because *everyone* was dressed up in cowboy-type things – even Fliss's mum.

"They should all come and enter the fancy-dress competition at the Open Day," I whispered to Rosie. "It'd be tough to pick a winner."

"Yeah, I'd no idea they all got so into it," she confided.

Now I must admit that country and western plinky-plonky music isn't my thing at all. But once it started playing and the caller started shouting out the dance moves, I kind of got into it. So did Kenny – but she got into it in a completely different direction from everybody else. When the rest of us were stomping forward she was doing a chasse to the side. When we did a mambo on our right, she did a pivot to her left. Disaster or what?

"Do try to keep up, Kenny!" Fliss hissed at one stage, but that only seemed to make things worse. Fortunately the adults round us were pretty forgiving, and I think she actually amused one or two of them as well.

"It's good to see you young ones throwing yourselves into it!" one older guy said as we were having a break.

"Throwing yourself into it is right, Kenny!" shrieked Frankie when he'd gone. "It's a wonder you haven't broken something yet."

"Like someone else's leg!" suggested Fliss.

"Well I might not be much good at the dancing," sniffed Kenny, "but I bet you I can

get the caller to come along to the Open Day
– for free!"

I have to be honest with you – the rest of
us had sort of forgotten that that's why we
had come. We were having such a laugh, it
had slipped our minds.

"Come on, then." Kenny dragged us to the
front of the hall. "There's no time like the
present."

We all felt dead embarrassed standing
there waiting for the caller, Ruth, to notice
us. She was going through a complicated
routine with someone and we didn't like to
disturb her. When she finally looked up she
gave us a big smile.

"Hi there! It's nice to see some new young
faces. Are you enjoying yourselves?" she
asked brightly.

"Yes, thanks!"

"It's great!"

"Brill!"

"It's so good, we wondered if you might
share this line-dancing with some more
people," Kenny asked seriously. "I don't
know if you've heard of Mrs McAllister's

riding stables? They were burnt down a while ago."

Ruth frowned sympathetically.

"Oh it's OK now, they've been rebuilt," Kenny continued. "And Mrs McAllister's having an Open Day on Saturday 28th. She lost a lot of business because of the fire, you see, and she needs to show everybody that she's up and running again. She might not be able to carry on if business doesn't pick up soon."

I shot Kenny a glance. I didn't think that Mrs McAllister would want everyone to know that she had money worries.

"And it would be dreadful if she did have to close down, because she does a lot of work for Riding for the Disabled. Rosie's brother goes, doesn't he Rosie?"

Rosie nodded.

"We were hoping to have some line-dancing at the Open Day, and as you're so good, we wondered if you might do the calling?" Kenny concluded innocently.

"Well…" Ruth spluttered. You could tell that she felt just like we had when Mrs

Chandri had steamrollered us with suggestions for the Open Day!

"Well, I guess I could pop in for an hour," she agreed at last.

"That's great!" We all leapt up and down.

"Here's Sita Chandri's number," Kenny pushed a piece of paper into her hand. "If you ring her, she'll give you all the details. Right then – are we ready to do some more of that bootin' scootin' stuff?"

I couldn't *believe* the nerve of that girl!

"Why did you give her Mrs Chandri's number?" Frankie demanded as we were walking away.

"I've just done the hard work in persuading her to come to the Open Day, haven't I?" Kenny explained patiently. "Now old Sita-chops will have to do all the boring work like arranging what time she has to get there. You know, 'details, details'." She mimicked Mrs Chandri. "We can't do everything, can we?"

The rest of us grinned. I think Mrs Chandri had probably met her match in Kenny.

So, we'd sorted out the line-dancing and

the lassoing competition. The fancy-dress competition would be easy-peasy to arrange. Now all we had left to sort out was the campfire cookout. It was time to launch Operation 'Cowboy Dad'!

CHAPTER FIVE

I arranged for everyone to come round to my place on Sunday so that we could start making the posters for the Open Day.

"But we haven't asked if anyone can cook round the campfire yet," Fliss reminded us. "So we won't be able to put that on the poster, will we?"

"Don't worry," I reassured her. "That's all in hand. The most important thing is that Andy is here at five o'clock to pick you up."

By the time everyone had arrived, I'd cleared the big kitchen table, covered it with newspaper and got out all my paints.

The Sleepover Club

"Hey cool, Lyndz – this looks great!" marvelled Frankie, dropping her bag to the floor.

"Let's hope our poster looks great when we've finished," I said. "I bet Mrs Chandri will make us do it again if she doesn't like it."

"Well, we'll just have to make sure it's perfect when she sees it then, won't we?" Frankie said sharply.

I poured us all a big glass of Coke and we settled down to work.

"I reckon we should stick pictures of cowboys and lassos and stuff round the edges of the poster," I suggested. "That way it will get people's attention and they'll stop to read what it says in the middle."

"Good idea!"

I gave everyone a piece of paper and we settled down to paint. I painted horses, and Kenny drew loads of lassos because she said that she was rubbish at doing people. We all cracked up when we saw one of Fliss's paintings. She said it was a line-dancer but it looked more like someone who was bursting to go to the toilet!

60

We were just picking which pictures we should cut out and stick round the edges of the poster when Stuart, my oldest brother, appeared.

"What are you lot up to, then?" he asked, peering over our shoulders. "You're not usually this quiet."

"Charming!" I laughed. "We're designing a poster for the Open Day at Mrs McAllister's stables, if you must know."

"Oh, right. What are all these?" Stuart was pointing to our drawings.

"Well there's going to be line-dancing and a lassoing competition and a fancy-dress competition," Fliss explained.

"You know what you need?" Stuart looked at us. "You need a Bucking Bronco. They're brilliant fun. You've got to hold on and it spins round faster and faster like those wild horses at American rodeos."

"What, you mean it's a real horse?" Fliss looked horrified.

"No Felicity, it's a metal one on a stand and someone controls the speed. They're excellent, trust me."

"Well that's all very well, Stu, but where are we going to get hold of one of those? For free?" I asked.

"Well sis, I might just be able to help you out there." Stuart looked very smug. "My friend Sam's father hires things like that out, and it just so happens that I'm going to be seeing Sam this evening."

"That's brill, Stu! Do you think he'll lend it to us?" I asked breathlessly.

"Yeah, Sam's father's a pretty cool dude!"

"Excellent!" I slapped Stuart hard on the back.

When he'd gone we were all *totally* hyper.

"This is going to be even better than we thought!" Rosie giggled.

We all settled down to work on the poster. We pasted the best of our designs round the edges, then it was time to write in the middle. After ages of deliberation (and arguments) we came up with this. Pretty good, huh?

WILD WEST OPEN DAY

at

McAllister's Riding Stables

Sandy Road

Little Wearing

Nr. Cuddington

on

Saturday 28th June

3pm onwards

Dress in your Wild West finery and enjoy:

Fancy-dress competitions

(Prizes for best child and best adult)

Lassoing competition

Line-dancing

Bucking Bronco

Cooking round a real campfire!

On Sunday 29th June
Pony trek at 10am

(Wear trousers and sensible boots)

Hard hats will be available from the stable

"How do you know about the pony trek on the Sunday?" asked Rosie when I'd written that bit in.

"Mrs McAllister told me about it when I went to the farm this morning," I explained. "She mentioned it before, but now it's official. It's the only thing she seemed really enthusiastic about, to be honest with you. Anyway, she's arranging the pony trek so it's nothing to do with us."

"But we will be going on it, won't we?" Kenny asked.

"Yeah, 'course!" I agreed.

Then I saw Fliss's face. She didn't say anything, but she didn't have to. She looked terrified! But I didn't have time to argue with her about that now. We had more important things to do. It was almost four-thirty and we had to start preparing for Operation 'Cowboy Dad'!

We all piled into the lounge and I put on a video. It was one of Dad's very favourite Westerns, starring this bloke called John Wayne.

"Aw man, what's this?" Kenny moaned.

"This is our secret weapon," I explained. "When your dads come in, you've got to pretend that you're really enjoying it, OK?"

Kenny made a being-sick face, and the others looked dead bored.

"Couldn't we just put it on when they come?" Rosie asked.

"Nope – I want them to think we've been watching it for ages."

We slumped back on the settee and watched. After what felt like an hour, the doorbell rang. I heard Dad answer it – then he came into the lounge with Frankie's father.

"Oh it's *True Grit*!" Dad exclaimed. "I love this film!"

"Me too," agreed Frankie's dad, and they both perched on the settee to watch.

Bingo! We all exchanged glances and carried on pretending we were totally absorbed in it too.

When Kenny's father appeared, Mum showed him through.

"Isn't this *True Grit*?" he asked, and settled down to watch as well.

Rosie's mum and Andy appeared at the same time, and they came into the lounge to join us.

"You're not watching a *Western*, are you?" Rosie's mum sounded horrified.

I flashed the others a look, and launched into Phase Two of the Plan.

"Wouldn't it be great to be a cowboy!" I said dreamily. "Riding the range on a horse all day..."

"Rounding up cattle..." Kenny continued.

"And cooking round a campfire at night," Frankie added.

"Yes, you're right there. No worries about anything," agreed Dad.

"No money worries," Andy added. "Just you, your horse and the open country. What could be better?"

Fliss looked as though she was going to get all huffy about her and her mum being better than that, but I shut her up with a glare.

"So, do you fancy cooking round an open fire then, Dad? And maybe telling some of your stories?" I asked innocently.

"Well, not now, Lyndsey," Dad laughed. "But I'd love to do it another time."

"What about you, Dad?" Frankie asked. "Would you do it? And you too, Dr McKenzie?"

"Are we talking about one of your sleepovers?" Dad asked cautiously.

"Sort of. Will you do it? Please!" I begged.

"I dare say we could rustle up some good campfire grub, couldn't we?" My dad looked at the other dads. "What do you say? Should we live like cowboys for an evening?"

"I don't see why not!" the others agreed, coming over all macho.

"Thanks Dad!" I leapt up from the settee. "You've just agreed to cook at the Open Day for Mrs McAllister's stables. You're a star!"

I hugged my dad and Frankie, Kenny and Fliss hugged theirs (well, Andy isn't Fliss's dad quite yet – he and her mum are getting married next month).

Rosie's mum burst out laughing and started to clap.

"Well done, girls! That was a fine piece of feminine trickery!"

The dads sighed and looked very sheepish.

"We were done there, good and proper!" Dad laughed. "Well, it's in a good cause I suppose!"

I took the poster down to the farm the next day, and was just giving it to Mrs McAllister when Mrs Chandri turned up. I was sure that she was going to find fault with it when I showed it to her, but she seemed really impressed. Ruth the line-dance caller had apparently already been in touch about the line-dancing, and Mrs Chandri asked me to give Stuart her number so that he could pass on the details of the Bucking Bronco.

"You've done very well!" she smiled. "And the posters will look stunning. I'll get them printed up as soon as possible. Shall I arrange to put them up, or do you want to do that?"

"No you can if that's OK," I smiled back at her. I remembered all too clearly the problems we'd had putting up posters in the past…

"Right then. I'll get in touch with you nearer the time, and we'll go over the details," she told me. "I think this Open Day is going to be a big success. Well done!"

Right up until the Open Day itself, all the planning went smoothly. *Too* smoothly. Mrs Chandri had estimated how many people she thought would turn up, and had bought food and drink at a discount rate. She'd sorted out prizes for the competitions and we'd helped to build the enormous campfire with our fathers. (I think they were still a bit miffed that we'd conned them like that, but they were kind of excited about it too, you could tell.) Ruth had checked out the stable yard and told Mrs Chandri where she wanted to put her stuff for the line-dancing, and they'd even rigged up a special sound system too. And Stuart had delivered the Bucking Bronco and a whole pile of crash mats to land on. Did this sound too easy or what?

The night before the Open Day, we all went down to the stables. The whole thing looked pretty awesome.

"This is going to be *so* cool!" we giggled.

"And don't forget we've got the sleepover to look forward to as well," I reminded the others. "So don't forget all your sleepover goodies, will you?"

As if!

The next day we got to the stables by two o'clock. It was humming with activity, but Mrs McAllister was pacing about looking very anxious.

"I'm sure it's going to rain," she moaned. "And what will we do then? The whole day will be a complete washout!"

"I'm sure it won't," I tried to reassure her. "Look, the sun's starting to shine. Shall we just put our stuff in the barn?"

She nodded weakly.

"Crikey, she's not much fun, is she?" Kenny moaned. "All that effort we've put into arranging this and she doesn't seem grateful at all!"

"I'm sure she's just anxious," I said, flinging open the barn door.

It was very dark inside, and smelt of warm hay.

"Come on! Make yourselves at home!" I giggled, running up the large straw bales which were piled up in one corner.

The others stepped in gingerly. Suddenly Fliss started to scream.

"I'm not sleeping in here!" she yelled. "Not with *that* thing around!"

CHAPTER SIX

Now if someone said that to you, you'd be expecting a one-eyed monster at the very least, wouldn't you? Well there was no monster there, only Alfie.

"Hello, boy! What are you doing here?" I rushed over to stroke his muzzle. "Don't you want to be involved in the Open Day then?"

"Never mind 'doesn't *he* want to be involved in the Open Day'!" snorted Fliss. "*I* don't want him to be involved in our sleepover!"

"You did agree to that, Lyndz," Frankie joined in.

"Hey guys." I pulled myself away from Alfie and turned to face the others. "This is nothing to do with me. We'll have to ask Mrs McAllister what's going on. There must be a reason why he's here. This isn't where he usually stays."

"I wouldn't fancy your chances with Mrs McGrumpy-Boots at the moment," moaned Kenny. "She'll probably bite your head off."

We all looked out on to the yard where Mrs McAllister was tearing a strip off one of the men who was setting up the speaker system for the line-dancing.

"See what you mean!" I mumbled.

"Hey look, Lyndz – your dad's here!" Rosie suddenly squealed. "What *does* he look like?!"

Sure enough, Dad was striding across the yard to the far field where a section had been cordoned off for the campfire. He was wearing his jeans and a checked shirt – and on his head was the biggest cowboy hat you've ever seen.

"Oh no, my dad's here too," Frankie cringed.

He was wearing the wackiest pair of cowboy boots on the planet. Talk about embarrassing.

"Where have they dug those up from, then?" Kenny was killing herself laughing.

"They are a bit, erm, *loud*, aren't they?" Fliss screwed her nose up in disgust.

"At least they're entering into the spirit of things," I said defensively. "Which is more than I can say for you lot. I thought we were supposed to be dressing up in Wild West stuff?"

I was wearing my favourite jeans with the leather chaps over the top, and had a cowboy hat among my sleepover things.

"I thought I'd be a Leicester City cowboy," grinned Kenny, slapping her jean-covered thigh and straightening her football top.

I suppose the others did sort of look like cowboys, because they were wearing jeans, checked shirts and waistcoats. They looked much better when they'd put on the cowboy hats they'd brought too. All except for Fliss, of course.

She ran over to her sleepover stuff and

pulled something out of a carrier bag. It was a full denim skirt with loads of white petticoats underneath, a suede waistcoat, lace-up boots and a hat.

"Hey cool, Fliss!" we all marvelled.

"But shouldn't you be *wearing* it?" I asked her. "I mean, that *is* kind of the idea of dressing up, you know."

Fliss shot me a look and began to wriggle out of her jeans. She must have forgotten that Alfie was there, because she gave an almighty jump when he whinnied.

"I'm not getting changed in front of *him*!" she snorted.

As if Alfie cared! Anyway, she made us stand in a circle round her so that he couldn't peek. Crazy or what!!

She'd just donned her very stylish pair of boots when Mrs Chandri came rushing into the stable.

"Oh, there you are, girls!" she panted. "We're nearly ready for the off. Can two of you help Mrs McAllister with the entrance money? And the rest of you come with me to check that everything else is in place?"

"You and Rosie help with the door money, Fliss," Frankie said, going into hyper-organisation mode. "And the rest of us can help Mrs Chandri."

Fliss and Rosie headed off to the entrance, where a queue was starting to form. The rest of us followed Mrs Chandri. The horses were already out in Mr Brocklehurst's field, so I couldn't understand why Alfie wasn't with them. I would have to ask Mrs McAllister later.

In the field away from the stable block, Dad was busy lighting the fire with Frankie's dad. Andy had appeared too. They were pretending to be cowboys and looked like they were having a blast. The line-dancing area had been set up and someone was testing the microphone. And Stuart was having a go on the Bucking Bronco, watched by a girl with short blonde hair.

Before I could investigate Stu's situation further, Mrs Chandri told us:

"We'll start with the fancy-dress competitions over here." She waved an arm in front of the new stable blocks. "Mrs

McAllister is keen to show as many people round the new buildings as possible, so do try to encourage people to have a look at them. Oh look – our first arrivals are here. Let's go to welcome them!"

She walked briskly down towards the entrance, leaving the rest of us to trot after her.

To be honest, we didn't really know what we should be doing. It was all right for her to smile at people and tell them how nice it was to see them, because she was sort of a celebrity around Cuddington. All we could do was stand there and look dumb, like a load of spare parts. At least there were loads of people pouring through the gates, which seemed to have cheered Mrs McAllister up. Unfortunately, you couldn't really say the same for Fliss, who was looking frazzled beyond belief. Maybe it wasn't such a good idea of Frankie's to have made her take the entrance money, because Flissy's not that great at maths.

When Frankie's mum appeared, she volunteered to take over collecting admission money, so Fliss and Rosie came over to join us.

"What's up, Fliss?" we asked.

She was the colour of a beetroot and looked just about ready to cry.

"It's those stupid M&Ms!" she spluttered.

"They're not here, are they?" we gasped.

"They sure are," Rosie told us grimly. "And they look as though they mean to cause trouble. They were very rude about Fliss's costume and were just about to threaten us when Mrs McAllister asked if everything was all right. We're going to have to watch them."

"Don't worry – we will!" Kenny said menacingly. "Or maybe it should be *them* who should watch out for *us*."

Before we could ask what she meant, a whistling pierced the air. Mrs Chandri's voice began to float towards us from across the yard. She was obviously addressing everyone on the microphone, so we went to join the crowd who had gathered round her. I don't think we really paid too much attention to what she was saying – we were too busy trying to spot the M&Ms.

Unfortunately I clocked them at just the moment when Mrs Chandri had thanked us by name for making the Open Day possible. We just sort of stood there like lemons whilst everyone applauded and the stupid M&Ms sniggered behind their hands.

When Mrs Chandri announced that the children's fancy-dress competition was about to take place, we huddled together and tried to decide on a plan of action.

"Whatever we do, we mustn't let them know we're having our sleepover here tonight," Frankie warned. "They'd try to spoil it for sure."

"We'll just have to put them off that scent," Rosie said. "What about luring them somewhere else?"

"Like the lassoing competition!" Kenny's eyes lit up. "Now that could be *very* entertaining!"

We walked over to the show-ring, where Mrs McAllister often teaches. It had been marked out for the lassoing competition with lines at various distances. Standing on the first line was a papier mâché cow, which

Stuart had also managed to borrow from his mate Sam's father. (I don't know what kind of business that man is in, but it all seems pretty strange to me!) Dad and Frankie's dad were there practising with the lassos.

"Look at them – they're just like big kids!" I sighed.

"I heard that!" Dad turned round and grinned at us. "I guess it's the nearest we're ever going to get to being real cowboys, so we're just savouring the moment. Mrs Chandri asked if we'd help to organise the competition. You don't mind, do you? It's just that the campfire's already going but there's not much we can do until it's time to cook. And Kenny's dad said he'd keep his eye on it for a bit."

To tell you the truth, we were glad of the offer. Especially as the Gruesome Twosome had just appeared behind us, along with a few more people curious about the competition.

"Sure Dad, go for it!"

When a large enough crowd had gathered, Dad explained to everyone that the winner would be whoever managed to lasso the cow at the furthest distance. The prize was free videos for a month from the local video shop.

"Right, could all competitors line up in front of me please, and could all spectators please remain behind the fence," Dad ordered.

Kenny and Frankie lined up to take part. Rosie, Fliss and I went round the far side to watch. I'd practised at home, and I knew that I couldn't lasso an elephant if it was standing still in front of me!

Rosie nudged me. "Look who's joining in too!"

Emma Hughes had barged to the front of the queue, and her little sidekick Emily Berryman was standing round the other side of the ring opposite us. A group of older boys were taking part, plus three women who were obviously just having a laugh until the line-dancing started and a few men, including Andy.

The competition started with the boys. Two of them were very good and lassoed the cow after a couple of attempts, but the others were *hopeless*. They had their three tries and had to drop out of the competition! When it came to Kenny's turn, she lassoed it without even *looking* at it.

"I think she's been practising this at home, don't you?" muttered Fliss.

Frankie got it right on her third attempt. And so did Emma Hughes – worse luck.

In the next round the cow was moved further away. A load of people had dropped out, so we figured the competition would be over pretty quickly.

"That might be just as well," said Rosie, looking up to the sky. "I'm sure I felt a drop of rain just then."

The sky was looking very black.

"Come on Kenny, you can do it!" we yelled when it was her turn.

This time she did look at the target – and lassoed it first time. Unfortunately Frankie missed it completely, so she came to join us.

"I hope Emma Hughes misses, because she's winding Kenny up big time," she told us.

But unfortunately, Emma didn't.

By the time the cow was moved again, there was only Emma, Kenny, one of the boys and Andy left in. When it came to Kenny's turn, she turned to Emma and said:

"Why don't you go first?"

Emma looked unsure, but the drops of rain were bigger and coming down faster and you could tell that she just wanted to get out of there. She took the lasso and had her three attempts, but missed each time.

"Bad luck!" said Kenny sarcastically, taking the lasso from her.

As Emma started to run with Emily towards shelter, along with the rest of the crowd, Kenny turned and grinned.

"A moving target! Just what I like!"

She raised the lasso above her head *and aimed for the M&Ms*!

"No Kenny, *don't*!"

I could see disaster ahead! But obviously so could Andy, because he ran towards Kenny, knocking her off balance. She stumbled to the ground, the lasso on top of her.

"That wasn't a very smart move, Kenny," he told her gruffly, picking up the rope. "Get into the shelter now before you get soaked."

The rest of us pulled Kenny to her feet and started to run. If anyone else found out what Kenny had been about to do, she'd be in big trouble. But that wasn't the only trouble we were going to have to face, because everyone was running to shelter in the barn. OUR barn. Where all our sleepover stuff was.

"You don't suppose…" panted Rosie as we flew through the door.

But it was too late. There in the corner, standing over our sleeping bags, were the M&Ms, wearing their cheesiest, most sickening grins.

CHAPTER SEVEN

"What do we do now?" hissed Fliss through gritted teeth. "They're bound to sabotage our sleepover things, aren't they?"

"Well they can't do anything with all these people here, can they?" reasoned Frankie. "We'll just have to make sure that they're never alone in here, OK?"

We watched the M&Ms like hawks whilst we were all in the barn, which wasn't easy because people kept coming over to distract us. Like Fliss's mum, who came to coo over her precious baby Fliss and ask why she hadn't entered the fancy-dress competition.

"Because it's for *children*, Mum!" Fliss looked dead embarrassed.

"But you *are* a child, darling!" Mrs Sidebotham giggled, tweaking one of Fliss's perfect blonde plaits. "Anyway, I'm going to enter the adult competition, so one of us should win a prize today!"

The rest of us raised our eyes at each other. Poor Fliss – having a mother like that was as embarrassing as still liking *Teletubbies*.

"It's stopped raining, everyone!" Mrs Chandri suddenly called. "It was only a little shower. Could all contestants for the adult fancy-dress competition please make your way to the stable yard? And I hope you're all ready for some line-dancing, because that will be taking place shortly."

"Bye darling, I must get a good spot for the competition," Fliss's mum laughed as she dashed away. "See you later for the line-dancing!"

"See you later for the line-dancing!" mimicked two voices behind us. No prizes for guessing who *that* was.

"Oh, shut your faces!" snarled Kenny. "You're a couple of wusses, you are! I challenge you both to ride on the Bucking Bronco! And I bet I can stay on longer than the both of you put together!"

"Oh yeah?" retorted Emma Hughes. "It's funny how it's always *you* who challenges us, isn't it? Are the rest of your little friends wimps then?"

She looked menacingly at our faces.

"All right then – challenge any of us to the Bucking Bronco!" Kenny dared her. "We'll still whup the pants off you!"

"OK." Emma Hughes stared at us all steadily. "Who do you think we should choose, Em?"

Emily Berryman grinned in that stupid way she has. "It just has to be Felicity Wimpy-Knicks, doesn't it?"

They both started to cackle. Fliss went white, then she went red, and then she went white again. But to give her credit, she didn't start to cry or anything – she just swallowed hard a few times and whispered:

"You're on!"

"Hey, Fliss – way to go!" yelled Kenny, slapping her on the back. "Follow me for the Bucking Bronco challenge!"

She led us up the yard to the small paddock by the gate. A small fence had been put up in the shape of a square, and the grass inside was covered by blue crash-mats. A metal horse was standing in the middle of it. There was no-one else there, apart from Stuart and the same blonde girl I'd seen him with earlier.

When Stuart saw us, he groaned.

"I wondered when you lot were going to show up. This is my kid sister, Lyndsey." He blushed and smiled at the blonde girl. "And Lyndz, this is Sam!"

"Sam!" I yelled. "I thought Sam was a boy! I mean, I can see you're not, but…"

The others were all laughing at me, especially Sam.

"It's all right, I know what you mean!" she grinned. "I'm glad Dad could lend you the Bucking Bronco. These are ace stables. I thought I might come here to have a ride myself."

"Oh-oh, don't get her started on horses!" Stuart groaned in mock despair. "I take it you want a go on here, then?"

"Not all of us," Kenny explained. "Just Fliss and these two morons here."

The M&Ms seemed a tiny bit over-awed because Stuart was there.

"Oh, OK. Who's first then?" Stuart asked.

"Could I go?" Fliss whispered.

"Sure thing – on you go!"

It took Rosie and me *ages* to help Fliss get on the thing, weighed down as she was by all her petticoats. And she looked absolutely terrified as Stuart started it off.

"Hold on, Fliss!" we yelled.

"Keep it gentle, Stu!" I pleaded. "Fliss hates stuff like this!"

"Hey, that's not fair – he's got to do it the same for all of us!" Emma Hughes shouted indignantly.

Stuart shrugged and started to make the Bucking Bronco go faster and faster. Fliss slithered over the head, then fell back and clung on sideways over the saddle. She looked dead funny, but we knew we couldn't laugh. When she finally tipped off, she looked exhausted.

"Well done, Fliss!" Frankie shouted. "You stayed on for seventy-two seconds. That's not bad!"

Emily Berryman was up next. And you'll never believe this, but she fell off after *five seconds*. I mean, how pathetic is that!

"You've got to stay on for over a minute, Hughes. What do you make of that?" Kenny called.

"Piece of cake!" she yelled back and clambered on to the horse.

"I hate her attitude!" Kenny sniffed. "I think we should teach her a lesson, don't you? Can I have a go at controlling this thing, Stuart?"

"I don't know about that!" Stuart sounded a bit unsure.

"Oh give her a go, she's seen how it works!" laughed Sam, pushing my stupid brother out of the way. "I sense there's quite a lot at stake here!"

Kenny gleefully grabbed hold of the joystick controller and made the Bronco spin. It went slowly at first and you could see

Hughesy looking really smug. Then Kenny speeded it up so all you could see was a blur of legs and hair. Then she slowed it down, then speeded it up. Then it started twirling and whirling, and although Emma was still clinging on, she was going greener and greener.

"I think you'd better stop it, Kenny!" said Frankie anxiously.

"No way!" laughed Kenny wildly.

But she didn't have to stop it, because Emma Hughes suddenly flew off, stumbled to her feet – and threw up all over the mats.

"*Yeuch!*" we all groaned.

"That was your fault, McKenzie!" snarled Emily Berryman, who had gone to comfort her friend. "We're gonna get you for that!"

"Yeah, yeah!" laughed Kenny. "You and whose army! Right then – I feel like a line-dance. What about the rest of you?"

We ran giggling up to the yard, where country and western music had just struck up. Fliss's mum was in the middle of the front row, clutching a bottle of champagne and wearing a big smile.

"Look what I won, darling!" She waved the bottle at Fliss. "And Andy won the lassoing competition too, so we're really cleaning up today!"

"Maybe we should make her clean up Hughesy's sick, then!" mumbled Rosie. The rest of us cracked up, but fortunately Fliss hadn't heard.

The line-dancing was great fun, apart from being trampled by Kenny's great fairy feet. She has no sense of direction, that girl, but at least she was enthusiastic.

After a bit, we noticed that we were being watched by the M&Ms.

"They're obviously too scared to join in!" Fliss grinned.

"Well, we wouldn't want any more accidents, would we?" Frankie smirked.

But still, there was something about their expressions that made me uneasy.

After the line-dancing it was almost time for the campfire cookout. Dad, Frankie's dad and Andy were in their element, pulling out jacket potatoes which had been roasting in the fire, doling out beans from great tin billy-cans and handing round sizzling sausages.

"Now eat up, y'all. There's plenty more cooking round that there fire. Yes siree!" Dad was on top form.

"You're dad's really sad, Collins!" hissed Emma Hughes as she walked past us with a steaming plate piled high. "I'd be embarrassed if he was my father."

"Ignore her, Lyndz," Frankie told me. "She's only trying to wind you up."

"I can't believe she's eating so much," Fliss sniffed. "I can never face a mouthful if I've just been sick."

"I'm sure that's her second helping too," Rosie said.

"Greedy pig!" snorted Kenny.

After they'd eaten, people soon began to drift away.

"Don't forget the pony trek tomorrow if you're interested," Mrs McAllister reminded everyone as they left.

She certainly seemed much happier when she turned to us at last.

"Well, thank you girls – the day's been a great success! I've had lots of new people booking lessons and most of my old clients have come back too."

"Great!"

"Yes, thank you for all your help!" Mrs Chandri came over to us. "You can enjoy your sleepover now, once we've got all this lot cleared away."

We looked round. There were discarded cups and plates everywhere.

"A couple of your friends, Emma and Emily, helped to clear a few things away, which was very good of them," Mrs Chandri continued.

We looked at each other. She must have been talking about the M&Ms! They certainly weren't our friends and they certainly weren't good. Something was wrong. *Very* wrong...

CHAPTER EIGHT

"Maybe they were just trying to get into Mrs Chandri's good books or something," Rosie suggested. "You know how they like to suck up to people."

That was certainly true, but I still couldn't help feeling there was more to their sudden show of helpfulness. We looked around, but they'd definitely gone. In fact there were only our parents left, and they were on the point of going home too.

"We've killed the fire," Dad told us, "so there's no danger of it spreading."

"That's good!" Mrs McAllister smiled. "I

couldn't face any more burnt buildings, thank you very much!"

"You will be all right, won't you Felicity?" her mother asked anxiously. "I'm still not happy about you staying in that barn by yourselves."

"It's perfectly safe and I'm just next door," Mrs McAllister reassured her. "Besides, they've got their own protection in there. No harm will come to them, I promise."

Our own protection? I looked round, but the others looked as puzzled as I was.

Fliss's mum still didn't look convinced, but Andy steered her away.

"Callum's staying with a friend, you've got a bottle of champagne, and I've got a pass to rent a free video," he grinned. "We might as well have a good night in."

Mrs Sidebotham giggled, gave Fliss a kiss and almost skipped away.

"Ah, love's young dream!" sighed Dad, making everyone laugh. "Right you lot, try not to frighten the horses or keep Mrs McAllister awake. I'll pick you up tomorrow afternoon after the pony trek. Be good!"

When we'd all said goodbye to our parents, we started to collect up the dirty plates. Mrs Chandri had put big plastic sacks all round the stable yard, so it was just a case of throwing all the paper plates into them. Still, it was pretty yucky.

"I hate looking at cold baked beans," sniffed Rosie, screwing up her nose.

"I hate baked beans, full stop," groaned Kenny. Ever since she sat in a baked-bean bath after our scavenger hunt last month, she hasn't been able to look a bean in the eye!

We were all pretty relieved when we'd cleared up the last of the plates and cups. After waving goodbye to Mrs Chandri, we looked at each other excitedly.

"It's sleepover time!"

We couldn't wait to get into the barn.

"What did you mean about us having our own protection?" Fliss asked Mrs McAllister, who was leading the way.

"You've got Alfie, of course!" she smiled, flinging open the door. "He's better than a guard dog!"

"Oh no!" Fliss groaned. " I thought he'd be gone by now. I can't sleep with him in here!"

Mrs McAllister seemed a bit put out.

"Well, I'm afraid you're going to have to. His stable is full of the sound equipment which is being collected tomorrow morning. I couldn't risk him going in there. Besides, he's a touch lame at the moment and I wanted to stable him where I could keep an eye on him. That's why he's not down on Mr Brocklehurst's farm."

"So *that's* why he wasn't out in the field with the others earlier!" It all suddenly made sense.

"I just took him for a short walk around whilst you were eating," Mrs McAllister explained. "And don't worry – he's been mucked out so he's not too smelly, are you boy?" She gently stroked Alfie's muzzle.

Looking at Alfie's big beautiful eyes, I couldn't understand how anyone could be frightened of him. And looking at the others, they seemed to be softening too – even Fliss.

"Right then girls, have you got everything you need?" Mrs McAllister asked us.

We nodded.

"The light switch is just over here, but I've left a couple of torches by your things in case you need them. You can use the loos by the stable block, but remember that the security lights will come on whenever you cross the yard. Right then, sleep well. I'll see you in the morning!"

She closed the stable door behind her and we were left alone. With Alfie.

"I'm not sure about this," Fliss shivered. "I thought we'd be able to use Mrs McAllister's bathroom, not some crummy old toilets next to the stables."

"Hey, less of the crummy!" I dug her in the ribs. "They're brand new, they are. You should be more polite."

"Well I say we should use them now, before we get ready to snuggle down for the night," Frankie piped up.

"Good idea, Batman!" I agreed.

We all grabbed our toilet bags and headed across the yard. Mrs McAllister was certainly right about the security lights. They nearly blinded us!

"No danger of intruders here then!" said Kenny admiringly.

"Don't!" warned Fliss, who looked absolutely petrified.

The toilet block next to the stables was very clean, but…

"It's F…F…FREEZING!" squealed Rosie.

"Aaargh! The water's like ice!" complained Kenny.

Now we don't usually spend long on washing and brushing our teeth at the best of times. But I think that night we were all done in about two minutes flat. We ran back across the yard and the security lights came on full blast again. This time the horses, who were all back in their stables, poked their heads over the doors and started to neigh and snort.

"Crikey, is this noisy or what!" grumbled Rosie. "I'll never sleep with that racket!"

"Will you lot ever stop complaining?" I demanded as soon as we were back in the barn again with the door closed behind us.

"So-rree!" echoed the others.

"Come on guys, we're supposed to be

having fun here! Let's play a game or something to get us in the mood," I suggested. "What about 'last-one-on-the-haystack-has-to-kiss-Alfie'!"

We charged at the pile of hay in the corner, screaming and elbowing each other out of the way. I've never seen Fliss run so fast! You ought to have seen her plaits flying and the determined expression she had on her face! It made me laugh so much I couldn't run. And then I got the dreaded hiccups. I collapsed on the floor, giggling and hiccuping.

"Kiss Alfie! Kiss Alfie!" the others chanted from the pile of hay.

I walked over to Alfie's pen and tried to plant a smacker on his nose. But he was so scared by the dreadful noise I was making he turned away and I was left facing his bottom. It was dead funny and only made me hiccup more.

At least it had cheered the others up. They were really in a party mood now. We played chase, and our jousting game where we ride on each other's backs and try to knock the other team over. But we had to stop that when Alfie looked as though he wanted to join in too.

We were just catching our breath when the security lights went on outside. There was a small window at one side of the barn and suddenly light came flooding through it.

"There must be an intruder!" squealed Fliss, leaping to her feet. "What are we going to do?"

"Maybe it's a fox or something," said Frankie calmly, although looking at her face I could tell that she was scared too.

We all huddled together. Then something started rattling the stable door. The handle started to turn. And we started to scream.

"AAARRRGGHH!"

"Goodness gracious me! What on earth's all that racket about?" Mrs McAllister was standing there, looking really shocked and kind of angry.

"S...sorry. We thought you were an intruder!" I explained, when my heart had stopped thudding.

Mrs McAllister's face softened.

"I didn't mean to startle you. I just came to check that everything was all right!"

"We're fine now," Frankie reassured her.

"Well, I think maybe it's time you were getting to sleep," Mrs McAllister told us. "You're going to have to be bright and alert for the pony trek tomorrow. I don't want any of you being too tired to concentrate. Night then!"

She shut the door behind her.

"I...I'd forgotten about the pony trek," Fliss stammered when she'd gone. "I might ring Mum up in the morning and ask her to pick me up early. I don't want to do it."

Kenny sighed in exasperation, but Rosie said quickly:

"I'm starving! Let's have our midnight feast now!"

"Should we get undressed and into our sleeping bags first?" I asked.

"Nah!" said Frankie and Kenny together.

We each went to find the goodies we'd brought for our feast. But funnily enough, there didn't seem to be as much as we'd thought.

"I could have sworn I'd brought more mini Kit-Kats," grumbled Rosie. "You lot haven't been eating them, have you?"

"No way. I brought crisps for all of us, and now there are only two packets left," moaned Kenny.

We looked dejectedly at the depleted pile of goodies in front of us. Then Frankie suddenly piped up.

"I bet I know what's happened to them! The M&Ms were in here before us, remember. I bet you *anything* it was them who stole our things."

"The thieving little scum-bags!"

"No wonder Emma was sick!"

"Serves her right!"

"I'll get them back for this!" Kenny hissed, stuffing a handful of popcorn into her mouth.

"Well maybe they think we're even now, after the scavenger hunt," I suggested. "At least it means we won't have to keep looking over our shoulders every five minutes to see what they're up to."

The others nodded.

"That's true!"

We silently got undressed, with us having to shield Fliss from Alfie again! We laid loads of hay on the ground like a mattress. Then we dragged our sleeping bags into a circle, unzipped them and...

"UURGH, that's GROSS!"

"I'm going to be sick. This is DISGUSTING!"

As soon as we'd got into our sleeping bags we all leapt out of them again. Our pyjamas were covered in *nasty slimy congealed baked beans*!

"The M&Ms!" we all said together.

"*That* explains why they kept getting extra plates of food!" said Rosie, trying her best to scrape the mess off her nightclothes.

"And why they were so keen to help Mrs Chandri to clean up!" I reminded the others.

"They've done us good and proper this time!" sighed Frankie. "We can't sleep in our sleeping bags, we've no blankets, and we're miles from home. Brilliant!"

We huddled together on the pile of hay in the corner.

"Anybody got any suggestions?"

Nobody said anything for ages. Then

Kenny said clearly and menacingly:

"You know what this means, don't you? This means full-out WAR!"

CHAPTER NINE

But before we could even *begin* to get back at the M&Ms, we had to get some sleep. But that looked impossible. How on earth could we get any sleep when our sleeping bags were ruined?

"We'll have to put our clothes back on. At least they'll keep us warm," Frankie suggested.

But once we were back in our jeans and jumpers, we still had the problem of what we were going to lie on.

"I know!" I leapt up. "What about lying on horse blankets?"

"What about telling Mrs McAllister what's happened and seeing if we can sleep in her house?" mumbled Fliss wearily. "Or better still, phoning for our parents to collect us!"

"Where's your spirit of adventure, Fliss?" snapped Kenny. "It'll only panic our parents if we ring now. And Mrs McAllister would never trust us to do anything again if she thought we'd messed this up."

"But *we* haven't messed anything up," Fliss reminded her. "It was those stupid M&Ms."

"Don't remind me!" snarled Kenny.

Meanwhile I'd climbed into Alfie's stall and retrieved a couple of blankets.

"I'll have to go and get some from the other horses," I told the others.

"How are you going to do that without the security light going on?" Rosie asked.

"Well I can't," I agreed. "You lot will have to pretend to go to the loo, so if Mrs McAllister looks out she'll think that's why the light's gone on."

"Great idea!" agreed Frankie. "Right, what are we waiting for?"

We all crept out of the barn and across the yard. The lights came on with a blinding flash, and sure enough, a light went on inside Mrs McAllister's house.

"It's OK!" I called out when I saw her face at the window. "We're just going to the loo!"

Mrs McAllister just nodded, in a resigned kind of way. But we had to walk to the toilet block anyway, just in case she was still watching us. When we got there, we peeped round the wall to make sure that the light in her house had gone out. It had.

"Right you lot, keep watch," I hissed. "Frankie, you come with me and give me a leg up over the stable doors."

Fortunately the horses all know me, so they didn't totally freak when I suddenly appeared in their stables. And it was quite lucky because in the first stable I found four blankets all neatly piled up in the corner.

"Will this be enough?" I whispered, handing them over to Frankie, who was waiting outside.

"We could do with a couple more to go over the top of us," she hissed back.

I climbed over into Bramble's stable. All the time my heart was thudding inside my ribcage. If Mrs McAllister caught me, she'd think I was trying to steal something and she'd never let me near her stables again! I found two more blankets and handed them out to Frankie. Then we ran like crazy back to the barn, knees buckling beneath the weight of the blankets. As soon as the others saw us, they ran across the yard too.

"You were lucky there. Mrs McAllister's just appeared at the window again," Kenny gasped as they flew through the door.

"You don't think she saw *us*, do you?" I asked Frankie anxiously.

"Nah!"

It took ages for us to get settled. We put the blankets next to each other on the hay, then lay down and pulled the spare blankets over the top of us. They smelt of hay and horses, which I loved. But of course, Fliss started whingeing.

"If she doesn't shut up, I'm going to tell her there are rats in here," Kenny whispered.

"Don't you dare!" I whispered back.

* * *

I can't honestly say I slept much. And it was kind of a relief when the first strains of daylight started filtering in.

"That's the worst night's sleep I've ever had!" moaned Rosie, rubbing her eyes.

"Me too!" agreed the others.

"What's for breakfast, then?" asked Kenny.

Breakfast! We hadn't even *thought* about that. Usually we sleep over at each other's houses, so we just grab something there.

"Oh, don't tell me we're going to be starving as well as sleepy when we go on this pony trek!" moaned Rosie.

That was all the excuse Fliss needed to let her go home. Or so she thought!

When we went across the yard to have a wash, there was a *fabulous* smell of eggs, bacon and toast wafting on the air.

"I hope you're hungry, girls," Mrs McAllister called out from her kitchen. "Because I've cooked enough here to feed an army!"

That was the best news in the world! *And* it was the best breakfast ever.

"You'll have to stay for the pony trek now, Fliss!" we teased her. "Because you'll have to work off that breakfast!"

"Of course Felicity is staying!" Mrs McAllister sounded very indignant. "I've told her before that she has the making of a fine horsewoman!"

Fliss blushed and looked dead chuffed. The rest of us rolled our eyes. Mrs McAllister had told her the same thing when she'd managed to cling on to the runaway horse at the Stable Open Day, and she'd not shut up about it for weeks! Still, it meant that Fliss wouldn't dare wimp out of the pony trek now.

When the trek was about to start, we were in the stable yard wondering how many people were going to turn up, when a voice piped up behind us.

"Sleep well, did you?"

The M&Ms! I couldn't believe that they'd dared to show their faces again.

"You'd better watch it!" Kenny narrowed her eyes and pointed a menacing finger at them. "I'm going to have you!"

"Oooh! We're so scared!" the stupid M&Ms pretended to quiver.

If Mrs McAllister hadn't started to speak, I swear that Kenny would probably have pulverised them, she was so mad.

"The most important thing is that everyone wears a hard hat," Mrs McAllister was saying. "No-one in my stable is ever allowed on a horse without one. I have a box of them here, and Miranda and I will make sure that everyone is wearing one which fits correctly."

Miranda helps Mrs McAllister around the stables a lot, and she was riding with us on the trek. So whilst she and Mrs McAllister kitted everyone out with a suitable hat, the rest of us looked round again.

Nine people had turned up for the pony trek, plus Mrs McAllister and Miranda of course. There were just two other people besides us and the M&Ms. They were two girls who seemed nice enough and about our age, but they were a bit shy and just talked to each other.

When we all had a hat, Mrs McAllister sorted out the ponies. I had Bramble, who I'm sort of used to riding. Frankie was on Marvel, Kenny had Trojan, Rosie was on Bailey, and Mrs McAllister put Fliss on Snowflake because she's ever so gentle and a real poppet. Then she divided us into two groups, and kept the five of us together which was really cool. Mind you, I never thought we'd ever get anywhere because Fliss took so long to actually mount Snowflake. I could hear the M&Ms spluttering from their horses, and that really put Fliss off.

"Ignore them Fliss, they're just stupid morons!" Kenny told her very loudly.

Sensing that trouble was brewing, Mrs McAllister helped Fliss on to Snowflake and went to have a word with Miranda. Then she swung herself on to Sinbad, her own horse, and called:

"Right Lyndsey, you and your friends are coming with me. We're going to meet the others for lunch at Pike Brook. Stick together, and if anyone has a problem, shout!"

So off we set, with Fliss wobbling about all over the shop.

"Just relax," I told her. "You won't fall off!"

"Don't even mention it!" she hissed back.

We started off walking slowly across the fields. Then we went into the valley, where we had a brilliant view of the countryside. There were birds and butterflies and all kinds of flowers, the kind of things you see every day but never really notice.

"Isn't this brilliant!" I marvelled, and I could tell that the others thought so too. Even Fliss looked more relaxed and was smiling into the sunshine.

When we started to climb up a gentle slope, Fliss went all ashen again. But when she realised that Snowflake was used to that kind of terrain, she relaxed into it and started to enjoy herself.

I couldn't believe it when Mrs McAllister called:

"We're almost at Pike Brook now!"

We'd been riding for an hour or more and it only felt like ten minutes! We could see the others ahead of us, and it was as though a weight had suddenly dropped on to my shoulders. I had actually forgotten all about the M&Ms.

Mrs McAllister brought us to a halt in front of the gurgling waters of Pike Brook. When we'd dismounted and handed over our reins so that Mrs McAllister and Miranda could secure the horses, we all took off our hats.

Then Kenny pulled the five of us together.

"This is an ace place to get our own back on the M&Ms," she said. "I've got a plan. All you've got to do is distract them when I give you the nod. OK?"

"Sure!" we all agreed, not knowing quite what we were agreeing to.

Mrs McAllister took loads of packets of sandwiches from her saddle-bags, and Miranda handed round cups of squash. We all sat down on the banks of the brook with our hats beside us, munching into our food.

"It's certainly thirsty work, this riding!" Fliss giggled, glugging down her drink. "I kind of enjoyed it though. I must be a natural rider after all!"

"You! A natural rider! Do me a favour!" The

M&Ms had wandered over. "You'd be more natural riding 'My Little Pony'. That's made just for little girls like you!"

While they were talking, Kenny had somehow manoeuvred herself behind the Gruesome Twosome and was nodding furiously. At first I thought she was agreeing with them – but then I realised she was trying to put her plan into operation.

"Well you should know!" I snapped back. "I thought your cupboards would be full of toys like that. It was a pretty childish trick you pulled last night."

"Oh, you liked that, did you!" smirked Emma Hughes. "I thought 'now what can I do to make their cosy little sleepover even better'!"

"And we thought you'd like some nice cold beans to keep you going!" chortled Emma Berryman gruffly.

"You're pathetic, you know that?" snapped Frankie. "It's time you grew up!"

"Is everything all right over here?" Mrs McAllister must have been alerted by the raised voices. "Where's Kenny?"

"I'm here!" Kenny appeared behind her. "I was just rinsing out our cups in the brook!"

"That was good of you, thank you." Mrs McAllister took the plastic beakers from her. "Right everybody!" she clapped her hands. "Could you all please bring any rubbish to me and put your hats back on. Miranda and I will help you mount your horses if necessary, then we can make our way back to the stables."

When the M&Ms had gone, Kenny turned to us with a wicked gleam in her eye.

"This should be interesting!" she smirked.

CHAPTER TEN

"Will you two please get a move on? We're all waiting for you!" Mrs McAllister was glaring at the M&Ms.

The rest of us were all ready mounted on our horses and had been hanging around waiting for the Queen and the Goblin for ten minutes or more.

"I told you this would be good, didn't I?" hissed Kenny. "And look at Mrs McAllister's face! She's not a happy bunny!"

Indeed she was not. She was frowning and red in the face and looked MAD!

The M&Ms meanwhile were rummaging

about in the bushes next to the brook and muttering angrily to each other.

"You put them down, didn't you?"

"No, you did!"

Mrs McAllister swung herself down from Sinbad and stomped over to them.

"Right, I've just about had enough of this!" she told them crossly. "Where are your hats?"

"W...we don't know," admitted Emma sheepishly.

"What do you mean, *you don't know*?" stormed Mrs McAllister. "How can you possibly have lost them?"

Then Kenny suddenly piped up, cool as you like:

"Erm, Mrs McAllister? I can see something floating in the middle of the brook down there. And it looks like a couple of hard hats!"

I thought Mrs McAllister was going to blow a fuse. I really did.

"*What!*" she yelled. Then she went closer to the brook to investigate.

Sure enough, caught up in a tangle of

weeds in the middle of the water were two
very soggy riding hats.

"How on earth did they get there?" Mrs
McAllister fumed. "No, don't answer that!
The most important thing is getting them
out, and I know who's going to do that!"

She gestured for the M&Ms to follow her,
and walked with them downstream until they
were level with the hats. She took a stick and
tested the water with it.

"Well, luckily for you two it's quite shallow
here," she told them. "Now, in you go and
mind your step – the pebbles on the bottom
can be quite slippery."

For one moment, I thought Emma Hughes
was going to tell her that she wouldn't go in.
But she took one look at Mrs McAllister's
face and thought better of it. Very gingerly,
she stepped into the brook and waded out
into the middle. It was deeper than it looked,
and by the time she could reach the hats, the
water was up to her knees. Emily Berryman
picked her way behind Emma, and was so
busy trying to keep her balance that she
didn't see that her friend had stopped.

We nearly wet ourselves when we saw what happened next. Emma turned round with the hats and knocked into Emily, who was caught completely off-balance and slipped over. And as if *that* wasn't funny enough, Emily started flailing around – and knocked Emma over as well!

You ought to have seen them flapping about in the water. It was class! Mrs McAllister didn't seem to think so, because she had to wade in after them in case they drowned or something. When she hauled them out they were covered in weed and awful scuzzy slime!

"Nice one, Emma!" Kenny started to clap.

"Enjoy your trip?" jeered Frankie.

The rest of us were just creased up. Fliss was laughing so much that I thought she was going to fall off Snowflake. Unfortunately, Mrs McAllister was still not amused.

"That's enough!" she snapped. "The sooner we get back to the stables, the better. Miranda, you'd better walk back with these two." She gestured to the M&Ms. "They can't ride back in that state. The rest of you come with me and stick together."

She swung herself back on to Sinbad and we set off.

All the way back we kept spluttering at the thought of the M&Ms in the brook. It had even been worth that uncomfortable night under the horse blankets!

We got back to the stables *ages* before the M&Ms. And by the time they appeared over the horizon, we'd taken all the tack off the horses and were packed up and waiting for Dad. They looked furious *and* uncomfortable by the time they came dripping into the stable yard.

"I'm going to tell my mum about this!" whimpered Emily Berryman.

"Good!" Mrs McAllister appeared out of one of the stables. "Because I intend to tell *both* your parents what disruptive influences you are. I should have known better than to let you come on the pony trek to start with. It was you two who caused all that trouble at my Stable Fun Day last year, wasn't it?"

The M&Ms looked guiltily at the ground

and began to shuffle their feet in embarrassment.

"Well, I don't want to see either of you anywhere near these stables again. Is that understood?" Mrs McAllister was eyeing them sharply.

The M&Ms had bright pink cheeks by this time, and looked as though they were about to burst into tears at any minute.

"*Is that understood?*" Mrs McAllister repeated.

They both nodded.

"Good!"

Mrs McAllister took the horses from Miranda and led them into one of the stables. The rest of us looked at each other. The M&Ms had been so totally humiliated there didn't seem to be anything left to add. We just stood and grinned as they slunk off down the yard to wait for Emma's mum to pick them up.

"Did you have a good time, girls?" Dad asked breezily when he drew up in the van.

"Brilliant!" we squealed.

"Excellent!"

"The best!"

"So did you sleep well?" Dad asked as he drove out of the stable yard, waving to Mrs McAllister as he left.

"Not really!" we spluttered.

Dad looked at us and shook his head.

"Well, was the pony trek good?"

"Great!" Kenny piped up. "And the M&Ms found it very refreshing!"

Well, we just lost the plot then. My sides were aching so much by the time I got home that I had to go upstairs to lie down. That just had to have been one of our best sleepovers ever!

When we went down to the stables a few days later, Mrs McAllister had calmed down and was in a brilliant mood. Loads of people from the Open Day had rung to confirm bookings for their riding lessons, and she said she was fully booked for a few weeks.

"That's fantastic!" we told her.

"Thanks to you!" she grinned. "Mrs Chandri and I have a little something for you to thank you for all your help with the Open Day."

She went into the house and returned with five small boxes. She handed one to each of us. Inside there was a bright shiny sheriff's badge which read: *You're a STAR!* They were so cool!

"Thank you!" we all gasped.

Mrs McAllister grinned.

"So with all this new business coming in, I might need a bit more help around the place," she continued. "Any offers?"

"Sorry, got to go!" The others started running off up the yard.

"Hey guys! Come back!" I called after them. "It'll be fun! Honest!"

Actually they were only joking, and they've been down at the stables a lot recently. Fliss actually enjoys grooming the horses now, which is a major achievement. But they all still refuse to help me with the mucking out!

Look, we're nearly at the stables now and I can hear the others from here. That Kenny's got a voice like a foghorn! And ever since Frankie got her sheriff's badge, power seems to have gone to her head even more than usual! Fliss will still be swanning around pretending she's a cowgirl and Rosie will probably just be taking it easy and grinning, knowing that the M&Ms won't be anywhere around. Bliss!

Anyway pardn'r, I'm goin' to round 'em all up and try to persuade 'em to ride the range with me. It's a tough life being a cowboy, you know!

Bye y'all!

31

The Sleepover Club Bridesmaids

Da, da, da-da! Wedding bells are ringing for Fliss's mum and Andy, and Fliss and the rest of the gang are bridesmaids! But when Fliss walks under a ladder and breaks a mirror, everything goes wrong. Fliss's mum starts acting strangely, and Andy's mum is bossing everyone around. Worst of all, Amber, freshly arrived from LA, is lording it over everyone, and Fliss's mum wants her to be a bridesmaid too. So who is going to be left out...?

Grab a bouquet and stroll up the aisle!